The Adventures of Zelda: A Pug Tale

The Adventures of Zelda: A Pug Tale

Kristen Otte

The Adventures of Zelda: A Pug Tale

Second Edition: December 2014

Cover Design: Michael McFarland

ISBN: 1491071664
ISBN-13: 978-1491071663

Dedicated to my stepfather, Jim, a kind and generous man who is missed greatly.

Table of Contents

Chapter 1
Beginnings

I spent my first two years in a small, crowded house with a woman, her four children, her boyfriend, and three other pugs. I was the smallest of the pugs, so I struggled to eat my share of food. While the other pugs slept, I crept out of the cage to find scraps. Eating was the only reason I left my cage because the man of the house was terribly mean. He yelled often, so I stayed in the cage, scared of his reaction if I stepped in his way.

Those first two years of my life were a blur, and every night I dreamed of a better life–a life with an endless supply of food, space to run, and friends to love. I never expected my dream to come true, but it did.

The day my life changed started like any other. After a typical morning of sleep, I woke up to the woman entering the house. Instead of ignoring me, she walked to my cage and lifted me into her arms. She carried me outside and placed me in the arms of a stranger–a woman I had never seen. This woman stood next to a man with a big smile.

Confused and scared, I didn't know how to react, so I went limp in this woman's arms. She carried me into a car, and the man drove us away from my old home.

I don't know how Hannah and Nate found me that day, but I am glad they did. Hannah, Nate, Lucy, and Ben are my new family. Hannah and Nate are the woman and man who rescued me from my old home. Ben and Lucy are their kids. Ben is loud, energetic, and about half the size of Nate. I play many games with Ben. Lucy is much smaller than Ben, but she is super cute, and I love snuggling with her at night.

"Why is she so wrinkly, Dad?" Lucy asked, the first day I came home.

"Because she's a pug," Nate said.

"Do all pugs have wrinkles?" she asked.

"Yes, they do. That's what makes them special. That and the smashed face," Nate said.

"I think her wrinkles are cute," Lucy said. When Lucy said those words, I knew she would be a great friend.

My new family calls me Zelda. I spend my days roaming the house, sleeping, eating, sleeping some more, playing, sneezing and snorting, barking at other dogs, and going for walks. I haven't seen an empty food bowl yet, and I am free to roam the house. I can't remember the last time I was locked up in my crate! Instead, my family and I play with my angry bird, my owl, tennis balls, and any other toy I can find. When I am super excited, I run full speed laps through the house. My family calls the laps pug sprints.

Walks are a brand new adventure for me. When Hannah or Nate put on their shoes, I know it's time for a walk. I run in circles around Hannah or Nate, trying to avoid the harness, but they always catch me. I don't mind the harness. I run in circles because I am so excited to go for a walk.

When the front door opens, I bolt down the porch steps, pulling Nate or Hannah with me. I step on the grass and sneeze five or six times. Despite the sneezes, I love the fresh air and the never-ending scents. During our walks, I run from one edge of the sidewalk to the other. On a good day, the squirrels run across the grass and up the trees. If I wasn't leashed, I know I could catch one.

My favorite part of the day is when the darkness comes. I snuggle with Lucy or Ben and fall asleep with my best friends.

I am a lucky pug. When I wished for a better life, I never imagined my dream would come true, but my new life comes with challenges. I am not sure how to be a good pug in my new home. I want to make my family proud, but sometimes my stubborn pug instincts take control. Other days I want more freedom, more treats, or more friends. Is that too much to ask?

Chapter 2
Zelda and the Treat Bowl

From my seat at the table, I watch Hannah pour a bag of my treats into a little bowl. She places a lid on the bowl and leaves the bowl of treats on the kitchen table.

I can't believe she left the treats within my reach!

The treats smell delicious, and if I leap on the chair, then step on the table, I can reach the bowl. My family enforces a strict "no paws on the table" rule, but they don't have to know I broke it.

When my family leaves after dinner, I sprint to the kitchen. I leap on the chair and hoist myself onto the table. The bowl of treats is a few pug steps away. With the treats so close, my guilt disappears for breaking the "no paws on the table" rule. I sniff the bowl and feel a sneeze coming. I let loose. The force of the sneeze causes me to whack my nose on the table.

Ouch.

I shake my head and regain my focus. I try opening the lid with my paws, but I can't get any traction on the slippery table. My paws are sliding everywhere!

I bite at the lid next, attempting to free the treats, but my flat face makes it impossible to grip the lid. I try lifting the whole bowl, but the bowl is too heavy to hold in my little mouth. I am stumped. I don't know what to do next.

While I sit on my hind legs devising a plan, I hear the car pull into the driveway. I leap off the table, to the floor, and dash to my dog bed. As the door opens, I plop on my bed.

"Hey bug," Lucy says. Lucy calls me bug sometimes. I think it's because she can't say pug. I run to her and lick her face. Ben crosses through the doorway next. He grabs the bowl of treats and sits on the floor.

Treats!

I dash for the bowl, but Ben lifts it in the air seconds before I arrive. I'm in a full-speed sprint, and I can't stop in time–I tumble into

Ben's leg. I bounce off him and plant myself in a sitting position facing him, pretending nothing unusual happened.

"Down," Ben says. I lie flat on the floor, and Ben gives me a savory bacon treat. We practice sit, down, up, and leave it before Ben speaks a strange, new command.

"Shake." He reaches for my paw.

Shake! What is shake?

We practice shake a few more times. I learn that shake means to place my paw in Ben's hand. While we practice, the treat bowl taunts me. I need those treats!

"Up," Ben commands. As I stand on my hind paws, I think of an idea. The plan depends on the up command. When Ben says up, I will follow his directions. Ben knows I can only stand on my back paws for a short time. When I stand, I will walk forward to Ben and the treat bowl. After he gives me the treat, I will fall forward, land right in front of the treat bowl, grab the open bowl with my mouth, and dash under the bed with it. It's the perfect plan!

"Sit!" Ben says. I wonder how long he has been telling me to sit.

"Down!" I lie on the floor.

"Up!" Ben commands.

This is it!

I jump up, stand on my hind legs, stagger forward, lose my balance and fall. My front paws land on top of the treat bowl, sending the bowl flying into the air. The empty bowl lands a couple feet behind me and the treats scatter across the floor.

With Ben laughing, I know it's time to go for it. I inhale all the treats in front of me. I have eaten a dozen treats when the goose honking that haunts the pug species begins. My excitement, coupled with my small and flat nose, causes me to lose my breath. I make a terrible sound like a goose honk until I catch my breath.

"What's going on here?" Hannah asks. She walks into the living room from the back room. She glances at the treats scattered around the room. Scared, I run inside my crate.

"We had a little accident," Ben says.

"What kind of accident?" she asks.

"Zelda knocked over the bucket of treats," Ben mumbles. Hannah laughs and picks up some of the treats lying close to her.

"Okay, just don't let Zelda eat all the treats. She is a little pug, you know," Hannah says.

"Okay, Mom." Ben lets out a sigh of relief. Hannah walks back to the office.

"Here you go Zelda." Ben hands me all the treats on the floor. "Don't tell Mom I gave them to you."

I am shocked. I made a mess, but I didn't get in trouble, and I ate the bucket of treats. In my old house, this would have never happened. I am so happy to be a part of this family.

Chapter 3
Zelda vs. Vacuum

After a few weeks with my new family, my days fall into a pattern. Most nights, I sleep in Lucy's bed under the covers with her. Ben thrashes and kicks during the night, so I stay away from his bed. In the morning, I wake Lucy with a sneeze to her face. I never intend to sneeze in her face, but when I lick her, a sneeze overpowers me, and I let loose.

Nate, Ben, and Lucy leave in the morning after breakfast. After they leave, Hannah and I take our morning walk. After the walk, I nap for several hours. When the kids return home in the afternoon, the rest of my day begins.

This afternoon Hannah returns home with a giant box. She places the box in the corner of the living room. I sniff the box, but it has no traces of other animals or dogs. The box stays in the living room until Nate returns home later in the day. He opens the box and assembles the parts into a robot. I hear Nate call the assembled creation Vacuum.

Vacuum has a blue, square base with two back wheels. On top of the base is a clear cylinder with another blue cylinder inside. Sticking out from the cylinder is a long tube that thins toward the top end. Vacuum doesn't have eyes or arms.

Hannah moves Vacuum into the coat closet, but she leaves the door open a crack. I approach the closet slowly. I paw the door open to see if Vacuum is blocking the milk-bone slot. Almost every day a milk-bone appears in the slot with envelopes and paper. When I stand on my back paws, I can reach into the slot and grab the milk-bone with my mouth. Sometimes I rip apart the paper to get to the milk-bone, but I hide the mess under Ben's bed.

As I approach, Vacuum stands still. Even though Vacuum doesn't have eyes, she is staring at me, daring me to come closer. I bark, hoping to get a reaction. She does not respond. I bark louder. No response.

"Leave it!" Nate shouts.

Leave it? Oh man.

I don't want to get in trouble today. I turn and run to Nate, forgetting Vacuum for now.

The next day Hannah opens the coat closet and drags Vacuum into the living room. She pulls a long black cord out and plugs it into the wall. Vacuum comes to life with a horrible, deafening sound. I rub my ears against the floor to block the sound, but it doesn't work. I need the sound to stop. I can't function with the piercing noise.

I shake until I regain my bearings. Hannah and Vacuum glide through the living room from one side of the room to the other. I think Hannah is trying to push her away, but Vacuum pushes back.

What if Hannah is in danger?

My ears hurt, but I can't let my ears get in the way of saving Hannah. I run forward and chase Vacuum. I give her my loudest, fiercest bark. Vacuum does not stop. I nip and bite at her, but she keeps going. I chase her around the living room. The three of us run laps until the deafening noise disappears. I stand frozen in the middle of the living room.

Hannah takes the black cord out of the wall and moves Vacuum back to the coat closet. Vacuum does not make a sound.

What just happened?

I don't understand Vacuum. I don't know if she is trying to hurt Hannah, but Vacuum needs to understand I am the protector of this family. I walk to Vacuum, bark three times, and walk away.

For the next several days, Vacuum stays quiet in the closet. She doesn't move an inch when I retrieve my milk-bones, so I stop shaking when I walk into the closet.

My shakes return when Hannah moves Vacuum from the closet and pulls the cord out. I know trouble is coming.

Hannah and Vacuum move next to the living room couch. Hannah pulls a tube out from Vacuum and attaches an arm.

Wait a minute. Where did the arm come from?

I bark at Hannah, trying to warn her this is a bad idea. She ignores me.

My fear rises when I hear the terrible sound. Vacuum propels into motion. The tube starts swinging as Hannah drags the arm along the couch. A million ideas run through my head of how Vacuum will hurt Hannah. I need to save Hannah.

Vacuum approaches my spot on the other end of the couch. The arm continues to sweep back and forth. As the arm approaches, I notice the place where the arm connects into the tube. Her weak spot is the connection.

I dart for it and wrap my mouth around the tube. My small jaws barely fit around it, but I pull as hard as I can. Nothing moves. I hear Hannah yelling in the background, but I can't make out any of the words. The end of the arm must have attacked her. I put every last ounce of strength into the next yank. The arm bursts free from the tube.

I did it!

With the arm in my mouth, I bolt downstairs to the basement. I carry the arm into the back corner closet. I drop it on the floor, use my head to close the door and run back upstairs.

I hear no sound in the living room. I hope Hannah is safe. I creep around the corner. Vacuum is out of sight, but Hannah glares at me.

"Where did you put it?" Hannah asks. I stare at her blankly.

Doesn't she understand that I saved her life?

"Zelda, the Vacuum isn't going to hurt you," Hannah says.

That's right!

There's no way that Vacuum can hurt me because I destroyed her arm. I smile and let my tongue hang out. Vacuum can't stop this stubborn, flat-faced, and wrinkly pug.

Chapter 4
Zelda and the Skate Park

The sun is shining, the flowers are blooming, and a light breeze is blowing–it is a perfect spring day. The whole family is going for a walk. I can't hold back my excitement.

"Zelda, stay," Nate says. I ignore his plea, sprinting back and forth between Lucy and the door until he tackles me. He slips on my harness and opens the front door. I scamper out the door to Ben in the front yard. Nate hands my leash to him, and we take the lead.

After a few weeks of walks, I know my favorite route in the neighborhood. The route is a big loop packed with tall squirrel trees, barking dogs, and a school. Ben and I head in this direction. Lucy follows us on her wheels while Nate and Hannah lag behind. I chase a squirrel up a tree, bark at three dogs, and sniff more bushes than I can count before we reach the school.

"Do you want to go to the park?" Hannah asks in front of the school.

"Yes!" Lucy shouts. "Can I go to the playground?" I am not sure what the park is, but if Lucy wants to go, I'm all for it.

"Sure, dear," Hannah says.

"Can I take Zelda along the path while you are on the playground?" Ben asks.

"Sure, just stay within our sight," Nate says. Lucy, Nate, and Hannah walk away.

Ben leads me on an unknown sidewalk in the opposite direction. We walk behind the school to a fenced area. Inside, a few people hit yellow balls into a net. As we walk past, I bark a hello. The sidewalk leads us past another fenced section that is different from the last.

I stop in front of the fence, fascinated by the scene. Inside the fence are ramps and towers of different sizes with people riding up and down the ramps on boards with tiny wheels. The people stay on the smaller ramps, except for one brave guy. He tries the tallest ramp, but he ends up sliding down it on his butt.

My curly tail wags from one side to the other in excitement. I want to go in the fence and run around the ramps! I bet I could make it up the highest one.

I trot around the fence, looking for a way inside. On the opposite side, I see a young man leave. I pull Ben that way and see a gate into the fence. When we are within four pugs' length of the gate, I lunge forward.

"No, Zelda, this way!" Ben says. He pulls me to a path away from the play area. I lunge again, desperate to get in the fence, but Ben isn't letting me go.

"Not today, Zelda. Another day we can go into the skate park," he says. "I don't think Mom would approve of you in the skate park." I let my tail droop and follow him.

Within minutes, I forget about my skate park disappointment. The magic cure is the beautiful weather, active squirrels, and the long walk. We circle the path and regroup with Nate, Hannah, and Lucy for the walk home. When we return home, I am exhausted. I drink a bowl of water and collapse on the cool kitchen floor.

The next day, the beautiful weather disappears. A gloomy, gray sky takes over, and raindrops fall throughout the day. Nate and I wait inside for a break from the rain.

When the rain slows to a drizzle, we venture outside. Nate leads us on a short loop, so we aren't far from home if the rain returns. When we reach the school, the rain stops. I pull Nate across the street to the path in the back.

"Where are we going Zelda?" he asks. I lead him to the door of the skate park, and I scratch at the fence.

"Do you want to go in the skate park?" I scratch again.

"Okay Zelda, we can go in," Nate says.

Nate opens the door, and we walk inside. I start to run, but Nate pulls me back.

"Wait a second, Zelda." Nate shuts the door and unhooks my leash.

"Okay, you are free!" he says.

I run along the fence first, looking for exits, and stopping for new scents along the way. I discover clusters of incredible blends of smells in the corners of the fence.

After I circle the area, I run for the first ramp. It's one of the smallest ramps; I run to the top without a problem. From the top, I spot the tallest ramp inside the fence.

I run down the ramp, but I lose my footing on the slick surface. I slide for a few seconds until I regain my balance on the ground. I ignore the goof and keep running. I see the big ramp and go for it. About halfway up the ramp, I lose my footing again. Gravity is not on my side today. I slide to the bottom.

On the bottom of the ramp, I take a minute to let my breath return. I examine the ramp for dry spots, but none are in sight. Since a full-speed sprint failed, maybe a slower pace will improve my traction.

I run again. I keep my pace steady up the ramp, but I only make it a few steps further than last time. The rain starts to fall again. I know my time is running out. I run one more time up the ramp, but I am not close this time. I slide down the ramp, landing next to Nate's feet.

"Okay Zelda, time to go," he says. He leashes me, and we walk along the path home. The light rainfall turns into a downpour. We sprint the last block, but it doesn't matter. Nate and I are soaked. Hannah, Ben, and Lucy wait inside the house with towels for us.

"How was that walk?" Ben asks.

"Actually it was great until the last five minutes. We went to the skate park," Nate says.

"You did?"

"Yes, I let Zelda off the leash, and she had a blast running on the ramps. She tried to run up the tallest one, but the wet ramp held her back. She slid to the ground."

"I bet that was fun to watch," Hannah says.

"Yes it was."

"Wait, it's okay to let Zelda run in the skate park?" Ben asks.

"Sure, if nobody is there, I see no harm in it," Nate says.

"Awesome. Can I go with you next time?" Ben says.

"Of course son."

Three days pass before the sun and blue skies return. During our morning walk, Hannah steers me clear of the skate park, but with the wet ground, I don't mind.

During the day, I watch the sun burn the damp sidewalks dry from my seat on the couch. The sun heats our front room too, and Hannah opens a few windows to cool the house. The skate park must be dry.

In late afternoon, Hannah laces up her shoes. I am ready for my walk, but Hannah grabs the other leash. I follow her with a droopy tail to the backyard. After she brings me inside, Hannah packs up and leaves. Maybe

I can go to the skate park with Ben when he comes home.

A few hours later, Nate, Ben, and Lucy arrive home as the daylight is fading.

"Okay Zelda, let's go for a walk," he says. Those are the words I want to hear. Nate leashes me, and Ben puts on his shoes.

"Can I hold her, dad?" Ben asks.

"Sure, son," he says.

I lead us down a different street than our normal route to get to the skate park quicker. They follow my lead, and we arrive at the skate park within a few minutes.

The park is empty!

Ben leads me to the gate of the skate park.

"Alright pug, let's have some fun," Ben says.

He sets me free. I sprint around the ramps, and Ben chases me. We run to every corner, and I run up and down the ramps with ease, saving the big one for last. I stand in front of the ramp and look up. It is taller than I remember. I start to doubt myself before my pug stubbornness returns. I jog to the other side of the park. I turn and look at my target. It's go time.

I run as fast as my legs will carry my twelve-pound frame. I reach the beginning of the ramp and sprint harder. I run up and up and up until my wrinkles smash into the fence on the edge of the ramp.

I made it to the top!

I stand panting with my tongue hanging out. I ignore the pain in my forehead and look down at Ben.

"Good girl, Zelda! That was awesome!" Ben says. I smile. I knew I could get to the top of the ramp!

Chapter 5
Zelda vs. Tucker and Whitney

"**C**'mon, Zelda, it's time to go for a car ride," Ben says. He grabs my collar and leashes me. Hannah and Nate pace in and out of the house, loading bags into the car.

"Do you have Zelda?" Hannah asks.

"Yes Mom. Can we go?" Ben says.

"We're ready. Let's go!" Nate says. We walk out of the house. I jump into the car and ride in the back on Ben's lap. I look out the window until my eyes start to close.

I wake up to voices.

"What dear?" Hannah asks.

"Zelda is making funny noises," Lucy says.

"She's just dreaming and snoring dear. Don't worry about her," Hannah replies.

"How come I've never heard her snore?" Lucy asks.

"Because you are asleep too!" Hannah says.

"Oh." Lucy giggles.

I drift back to sleep. When I wake the second time, I hear dogs barking.

Dogs!

I stand on my front legs to look out the window. We park at a house with two dogs waiting inside the front door. Both dogs are a little bigger than me. The dog with short white fur and orange spots is barking with excitement. The second dog has long gray fur, a beard, and a menacing bark. Ben opens the door, and we walk to the front door.

"Hi Tucker," Nate says to the white dog. Nate bends over to greet Tucker. Tucker says hello with a long lick to Nate's face.

A man and a woman walk into the room. I remember Nate's mom and dad from their visit to our home. Ben and Lucy run to them, giving them a big hug.

"Did you have a good trip?" Nate's dad asks. I run to him and lick his hands as he pets me.

"Yep. The drive was quiet," Nate says.

"It's good to see you," Nate's mom says.

"Good to be here, Mom." Nate hugs his mom.

We move down the hallway into a big room in the back of the house. The gray dog sits on the end of the couch glaring at me. Lucy sits on the couch next to the gray dog and pets her.

"Hi Whitney," Lucy whispers.

I jump on the couch to say hello to Whitney. I sit next to her, but she doesn't move an inch or acknowledge my presence. Maybe she is tired or having a bad day.

I hop back to the floor and start exploring. In the corner of the room, I see a basket of toys. I grab the first one, a remnant of a stuffed squirrel. I bring it to Ben on the couch-he is always willing to play. Tucker sits beside Ben. With the squirrel in my mouth, I jump on the couch next to Tucker. When I land, Tucker growls.

Yikes!

I back away, not wanting any trouble, and leave the squirrel on the couch. I jump to the floor to explore the house instead. I trot through the hallway to investigate the bathroom and front room. My investigation comes up empty, but I like the long hallway. It is perfect for fetch and pug sprints.

I wander upstairs and find more bedrooms and a bathroom. I notice something strange in one room. Instead of a door, there is a gate.

What is in that room?

I look at the height of the gate. It's probably too high for me to jump over, but maybe if I had the right momentum...

"Zelda, what are you doing?" Lucy asks from the top of the steps. "Let's go downstairs." She tries to lift me up, but I squirm my way to solid ground.

"Fine, stay here," Lucy says and stomps down the stairs.

I follow her downstairs and troll the kitchen for scraps and snacks. I see two food bowls and a water bowl. The different food smells delicious. I will try some at dinner time. In the corner of the kitchen, I see a glass door. I look outside into the backyard.

"Do you want to go outside?" Nate asks. I sit by the door and look at him on the couch.

"Okay, I'll let you out," he says. Nate rises from the couch and opens the door without leashing me. I'm confused.

"Go ahead," he says, so I go.

I run out the door, down the deck steps, into the backyard. I sneeze twice, and then sprint through the yard. I quickly understand why Nate didn't leash me. Surrounding the yard is a tall white fence. Even though I'm trapped in a big square, I can run all over the yard, at super pug speed. I run from one corner to the other corner of the yard. My excitement grows and builds into a goose honking fit. When I recover, I take it easy and sniff the fence line.

This is great!

"C'mon Zelda, time to come back inside," Nate yells. I sprint back into the house. I grab a drink of water before curling up on the couch with Nate.

I awake an hour or two later, and I glance around the room. Nate and Hannah are in conversation with Nate's parents. Whitney is lying in the same spot on the couch. Tucker is out of sight, and I don't see the kids.

My stomach growls, so I wander to the food bowl. The new food tastes so good! Whitney follows me to the food bowl, so I grab another mouthful and take it to the living room to eat with the group. I finish my mouthful and walk back to the bowl, but Whitney is waiting for me. She won't let me near the food, baring her teeth when I come close. I try to sneak around the back, but she blocks my second attempt. I walk to the living room dejected and hungry.

Why don't these dogs like me?

I am starving the next morning. Lucy is fast asleep, so I go downstairs. I am the only creature awake. I beeline for the food bowl, relieved to see it filled. I chow down until I'm stuffed. As I finish my last bite, Hannah and Nate join me downstairs. The rest of the family comes a few minutes later.

"Who needs to go out?" Nate's mom asks.

Tucker, Whitney, and I run to the back door. She opens the door, and we sprint outside. Tucker races ahead. I follow him around the yard, in hopes he wants to play. I give up after a few laps and look for Whitney. She is nowhere in sight, probably inside already. I run a few more laps before Nate calls me inside.

Nate's mom brings out the basket of toys later in the day. I spring to her side, ready to play, along with Tucker and Whitney. She throws a ball down the hallway and all three of us sprint to the ball. I reach the ball first, snag it, and bring it back amidst growls from Tucker. Nate's mom throws the ball a second time. We run again, but I let Whitney retrieve the ball.

We play fetch a few more rounds, but I let Tucker and Whitney retrieve the ball to keep them happy. After a few rounds, I can't hold off any longer. On the next throw, I sprint as fast as I can for the ball. I am one step ahead of Tucker and Whitney. I grab the ball and run to Nate's mom, proudly displaying it in my mouth, as I run past the other two dogs. Tucker looks at me, but he doesn't make a sound.

On the next throw, I find myself head to head with Tucker in a race to the ball. Tucker inches me out with his longer snout and grabs it. My instincts kick in; I jump on him, and we roll on the carpet. As we roll and pant together, I know the tension is broken.

Tucker, Whitney, and I have no more scuffles. We go for a walk later in the day. We play fetch and run outside in the yard together. Whitney and I even eat side by side at dinner, so I know Tucker, Whitney, and I will become best friends.

The following morning Hannah and Nate pack our bags. I am sad to leave the fenced yard, long hallway, and my new friendship with Tucker and Whitney, but I know when I return, our adventures together will continue.

Chapter 6
Zelda Goes to School

When we enter the dog store parking lot, my heart skips a beat. The dog store is a pug paradise. Toys, treats, dog food, and tons of wonderful scents fill the aisles. I have even met dogs on past trips to the store! If I had to live anywhere besides my home, I'd pick the dog store.

After we walk into the store, I take Ben and Lucy into the toy aisle. When Hannah appears at the end of the aisle, I am checking the selection of bones.

"It's time for class," Hannah says and motions to the right.

Ben and Lucy bring me to strange corner of the dog store and enter a doorway. Inside the small room with short walls are several chairs, a few people, and two dogs.

Dogs!

I bark and lunge at the other dogs.

"Dad, help me," Ben pleads. Nate reaches for the leash.

"Okay. I have her," Nate says.

Nate pulls me to an empty corner, and the family follows. They sit in the chairs. I jump in Lucy's lap to study my surroundings. A black dog with floppy ears is sitting on the ground next to a man and woman. Another dog sits beside her owner, an older woman. The dog is dark brown with pointy ears. She is the biggest dog in the room, probably about seven pugs' worth. Another woman stands near the doorway.

"Okay, let's get started," says the woman at the doorway. "My name is Rebecca, and I'll be your instructor for the next 6 weeks. Let's have everyone introduce themselves and tell each other about your dogs."

Her voice is stern. She reminds me of the scary man from my old home. I sit and listen.

From the introductions, I learn the black dog, who is the size of five pugs, is a black lab mix named Bella. The other dog is a shepherd mix named Chloe. Both dogs are a year younger than me.

After the introductions, Rebecca approaches each dog, gives her a treat, and pets her. When she approaches me, I back under Nate's chair. I don't want to be near her. Her treat might be a mean trick.

Rebecca calls to me again, but I stay under the chair. She leaves the treat on the ground and walks away. I ignore the treat and hop back on Lucy's lap. I don't trust this Rebecca.

Rebecca talks to the group for a while, but I only pick up bits and pieces. I watch the other dogs, trying to get a read on them. I start to fall asleep when Hannah interrupts my slumber.

"Zelda, come here," she says. As I jump off Lucy, I hear a clicking noise across the room.

What was that?

I look around the room.

Click.

This time the click is next to me.

"Do you want a treat Zelda?" Nate asks. I turn to Nate and see a treat is in his hand. *How did I miss that?* I charge for the bacon strip.

Click.

The click is from behind Nate. Nate holds out another bacon strip. I grab it.

Click.

Nate hands me another treat. Curious, I look around the room and see a familiar pattern with Chloe and Bella. A click, then the owner treats the dog. Although the clicking noise is annoying, it's easy work for a treat. I eat four more treats before Rebecca interrupts us.

"Okay, your dog will now associate the clicker with treats and good things. Just remember, any time you click, you must treat. Let's move on to the basic command of sit." Rebecca turns to us and asks, "Does Zelda know sit?"

"Yes," Nate says.

"Great. Let's demonstrate the proper technique with her," Rebecca says. Rebecca takes my leash and leads me into the middle of the room. I back away from her as far as the leash allows.

"Zelda, sit," Rebecca commands. I smell the treat in her hand, but I don't trust her.

"Zelda, sit," she says again, glaring at me. I stand, resisting the urge to sit. She is not going to win this game.

"Zelda, sit." Rebecca pauses for a minute and keeps talking, "If your dog is being stubborn, do not reward or click her. Release her, walk away for a minute, return, and try again." Rebecca hands my leash to Hannah.

"Okay, let's try with Bella. Maybe I'll have better luck with her. Bella, sit." Bella follows the command and sits. *Click*. Rebecca hands Bella a treat.

"Perfect. Good job Bella," Rebecca says.

What!

I can't believe the game was that simple. Sitting for a treat? I can do that in my sleep. My stubbornness and fear cost me a treat. Maybe this Rebecca is not like the mean guy from my old home.

"Zelda, sit," Hannah says. I sit. Hannah clicks and treats me.

When we stop playing the sit-and-click treat game, my stomach feels like it is going to burst. I have never eaten so many treats in my life.

"That's all the time we have until the next class," Rebecca says.

"Okay Zelda, time to go," Hannah tells me. We walk with the crowd to the door. On our way, Chloe approaches from the opposite side. I make a rash decision to show I am the top dog, even if she is seven times the size of me. I bark and lunge at her before Nate pulls me to him.

"What was that?" Rebecca asks. "Do you have the small dog syndrome?"

Rebecca walks to me and squats down to my level. I back away, but she's too quick. She grabs my harness, so I can't move. With her other hand, she strokes my head. My defenses kick in. No strangers pet me. I only allow those I love to touch me. I feel my fur begin to stand on my back. I know I shouldn't bite her, so I do the only other thing I can. I sneeze, showering Rebecca's hand and face with snot. Upon snot impact, she releases me, dropping a treat before walking away.

I carefully walk to the treat, suspicious of Rebecca and the treat, but the treat smells like cheese. I look both ways. Rebecca is on the other side of the room, so I take the risk. I gobble it up. It's the right choice.

"C'mon Zelda," Hannah says.

My family guides me out of the store, steering clear of any other dogs. I wonder if I'll ever see Chloe, Bella, and Rebecca again. Didn't I hear Rebecca say something about next time?

Chapter 7
Zelda and the Vacation

"Let's go, Nate. We are going to be late," Hannah says.

"How can we be late to leave on our own vacation?" Nate replies.

"We are on a time schedule," she says and walks out the door.

"Let's go, Zelda," Nate says. "Before she leaves without us."

We walk to the car. I jump into Ben's lap in the back. I have no idea where we are going, but I am excited. I love trips, exploring new places, and discovering new smells. With a new adventure so close, I hop from one seat to another until Ben grabs me, pulling me close. I squirm, but he doesn't release his grip. I give up and relax my body.

We arrive at a strange house with familiar faces. I cannot place when or where I met the man and woman of the house, but I know we have met. I jump out of the car and run into the yard, dragging Ben and the leash behind me.

"Let's go inside," Hannah says.

"Are you sure we can't bring Zelda with us?" Ben asks.

"Sorry, Zelda can't go on vacation with us," Hannah says.

I follow my family into the house. When Ben unleashes me, I dash up the stairs to explore. The house is much bigger than ours. It has a full flight of stairs with lots of space for playing. The upstairs has a long hallway leading to three bedrooms. The living room, kitchen, and dining room are on the other side of the top floor. Scattered throughout the living room and kitchen are a few of my toys, my bed, and my bowls.

How did they get here?

I scamper down the stairs. The bottom floor has one main room with a big couch. The other two rooms are small and filled with boxes. Downstairs the air is damp and dark.

"Zelda, come here," Hannah calls from upstairs. I run up the stairs and find her in the kitchen.

"It's time for us to go," she says. "Say your goodbye to Zelda." Lucy bends over and scoops me up. She gives me a big squeeze.

"I'll miss you," Lucy says. She puts me back on the ground. Ben reaches down and pets me.

"See you later," Ben says. Hannah and Nate both give me a quick pet.

"See you in a week Zelda," Nate says. "Be good."

A week? What's happening?

"We will take good care of her," the woman says.

"Bye Zelda," Nate says. They walk down the stairs and out the door.

I run to the couch in the living room. I put my front paws on the windowsill and look out. I see my family get into the car without me.

I feel the panic rising inside, and I can't stop it. I double over and start heaving, trying to catch my breath.

"It's okay Zelda," the woman says. She pets my forehead wrinkles, and I finally stop goose honking.

"C'mon, Zelda, let's go downstairs," she says. I cannot believe my family left me, but I have nowhere else to go, so I follow her.

Downstairs, the man sits in a big chair and the woman sits on the couch. I find a comfy spot on the opposite end of the couch and lie down. One of the benefits of being a pug is I can sleep anywhere and anytime. Sleeping always makes me feel better.

I rise from my nap a few hours later with a grumbling stomach. I wander upstairs to my food bowl and find it full. I chow down, eating away my sorrows.

"Steve, can you take her out?" the woman asks. Steve must be his name. He gets up, puts on his shoes, leashes me, and takes me outside. I do my business before coming back inside.

"I'm going to bed Megan," Steve says.

"Okay, I'll be up soon," she replies. Bedtime sounds good to me. I follow Steve upstairs to the bedroom. There is no way I can make the jump onto this bed–it's too high. I walk over to Steve for some help. He ignores me and gets into bed. I lie on the floor next to the bed and wait for Megan.

She walks in a few minutes later. I give my best sad pug eyes, but she doesn't do anything.

"It's time to go to sleep," she says. Megan crawls into her bed. I walk into the living room and curl up on the couch alone.

The next day I lie on the couch in front of the big window, waiting for my family's return. They said they would be gone a week, but I can't remember how many dark sleeps are in a week. I think it's four or five dark sleeps, but I don't want to be away from my family for that long.

I barely move from my window seat on the couch over the next few days. On the fourth morning, I decide to stop sulking. Steve and Megan aren't as snuggly as Lucy, as playful as Ben, or as funny as Nate and Hannah, but they are sweet and treat me well. I stop window watching, and I follow Megan during the morning hours. When she grabs my leash, I run in circles around her feet. She understands my hint.

On our walk, a distinct dog smell fills my nose. It's not a common dog smell. I look to the house on my right.

What is that?

Standing two pug-lengths away from me is a gigantic canine. The dog is brown and white, with floppy ears and a droopy face. The dog's head is the size of my whole body, and the dog is almost as tall as Megan!

The dog shuffles its huge paws in our direction. I back away behind Megan, prompting her to turn around. She shrieks, and her whole body shudders.

"Oh my gosh! It's a Beethoven dog! C'mon, Zelda, let's go!" she says. She pulls me forward, but I race ahead to lead her away from the giant dog.

The remainder of the walk is uneventful, but my fur remains upright on my back from our encounter. When we return home, I am exhausted. I find a comfortable spot on the couch and lie down.

I fall asleep, but Beethoven visits me in my dreams. I am on a squirrel chase when Beethoven sneaks up and snatches the squirrel. In my next dream, I see Hannah and Nate sprinting in my direction away from Beethoven. I awake shaking. I don't want to dream anymore.

I get up and wander through the house. I realize nobody is home. I find my old spot in front of the window on the couch. The daylight is almost gone when Megan and Steve return home. I go downstairs and greet them with a friendly bark. We play with some tennis balls, and then I snuggle on the couch with Megan.

The next few days pass without any encounters with the giant dog, but we have avoided his house on our walks. I find myself enjoying the freedom of a bigger house and start to feel guilty. I wonder if my family is coming back. I go into the kitchen to listen to Megan.

"What time will they be here?" Steve asks.

"Around 7:00pm," Megan replies.

"Okay, I'll be home by then," Steve says.

Wait, does that mean my family is coming back?

I run three laps around the kitchen and living room. When I finish my laps, I leap on Megan's lap and lick her face.

"Are you excited for your family to come home?" she asks in between laughs. I lick her face again and bring her a toy.

The day goes by painfully slowly. I wait by the window hoping the car will arrive. When the car pulls into the driveway, I race down the steps to the door. I jump on the screen door; it pushes open. I sprint straight to the car, arriving as Nate opens the door. I leap in the car, landing on his lap.

"Well hello, Zelda!" Nate says with a smile. "Did you miss us?"

I lick his face before jumping to each seat and greeting my family with kisses, sneezes, and a wagging tail. My family is home. Life is good.

Chapter 8
Zelda vs. the Leaf Pile

From my perch on top of the couch, I watch the leaves blow from the trees, and the squirrels scurry through the yard. The hot and humid days of summer are gone for now, and the cool breeze feels great ruffling through my fur.

The weather is perfect for pug walking. I take long walks with the family in this weather. In the mornings, I walk with Hannah, and when Ben and Lucy return home in the afternoon, the family goes together.

This morning, Hannah finds her hoodie and yellow shoes, sits down, and ties her shoes. I run to her and grab the shoelaces with my mouth. I try to help her tie the yellow shoes, but she pushes me away. I wait by the door until she is ready.

We head out the door a couple minutes later; I veer to the left. Hannah follows my lead, and we turn right onto Edgewood–my favorite street. A canopy of large oak and maple trees line both sides of the street, creating shade on the sidewalks at any time of the day. The big trees attract squirrels and chipmunks–animals I love to chase. The houses are filled with dogs of all shapes and sizes.

My favorite spot on this street is a light post on the corner of Edgewood and Meadowfield. The light post sits at a popular intersection. With many dogs passing by the light post, every visit introduces me to a new smell. I love the light post. I lead the way down Edgewood, pulling Hannah along behind me.

Squirrel!

I spot the first squirrel midway down Edgewood. The squirrel is on the opposite side of the street, out of my reach, so I ignore its taunting. A second squirrel runs up a tree in the next yard on our side of the street. I charge forward, sprinting four strides before Hannah yanks me backward.

"Zelda, calm down!" Hannah yells. I ignore her and press forward. The tree is a few pug steps away.

I want that squirrel. It's so close.

When I reach the tree, the squirrel stands a few branches above me. I jump up and try to gain traction on the tree trunk.

"Let's go!" Hannah pulls me away from the tree and the squirrel. I walk a few paces and sit in the grass, disappointed. Hannah pleads with me to keep walking. I lie on the grass and look at the street ahead.

The light post!

I dart up and run towards the corner light post at the end of the street. As I approach the corner, I sneeze. Something isn't right. I don't smell the normal mix of dog scents, so I slow to a walk. Ahead, I see the source of the problem. Something is on top of the ground around the light post. I walk with caution to the corner.

As I approach the corner, I realize the barrier is a collection of leaves in one big pile. I stop and stare at the leaf pile. Why would anyone put a bunch of leaves in a pile? And why did they pile the leaves on my corner light post? Is the pile covering up something?

I step closer, sniffing to examine the pile, but my nose doesn't provide any hints about the leaf pile. Walking straight into the pile could be a trap. What if there are thorns in it?

I decide to ignore the leaf pile and the corner light post for today. It's too risky. I bet the pile will be gone tomorrow.

Hannah and I stroll past the elementary school and through the park. I see two more squirrels, but I don't catch either one. When we arrive home, I'm thirsty and tired. I drink a bowl of water and sprawl across the couch.

On our walks the next few days, I lead my family to the corner light post, but the leaf pile remains. Since the leaf pile seems permanent, I lead Nate in the opposite direction of our normal route, hoping to find a new favorite smell spot. We turn down Sunbrook. I haven't walked on Sunbrook in several days. Huge oak trees line the yards on Sunbrook, but the lack of dogs causes me to steer away from Sunbrook most days. I like streets with action and excitement.

While we walk down the street, I notice something strange in the distance. I pick up the pace; I recognize the similar shape. It's another leaf pile. Confused, I keep walking.

When we reach the corner of Sunbrook and Meadowfield, I turn left towards Edgewood.

When I turn the corner, I see another leaf pile. My excitement rises. Since more leaf piles have appeared, maybe the other leaf pile will be gone. We pass the elementary school, and Nate stops to talk to the man in the blinding yellow shirt. I want to see the light post. I bark and pull Nate forward.

We arrive at the corner light post, and my frustration returns at the sight of the leaf pile. I sigh, ignoring the squirrel running across the street. I am too distraught by the leaf piles everywhere. They surround fire hydrants, tree trunks, and light posts. I don't know what to do.

When we return home, Nate takes a seat on the couch and turns on the television. I curl up in his lap and fall asleep, trying to forget about the leaf piles.

I awake later in the afternoon. I feel refreshed and light-hearted from my nap. Nate asks if I want to go outside. I answer by waiting at the front door. He takes me out to the backyard. I notice the grass is covered with red, yellow, and orange leaves. I hear a noise and look at the next yard over. I see Don, our neighbor, working outside in his flower beds. He rakes the leaves out of the flower beds into a pile.

He's making a leaf pile!

I dash in the direction of the front yard, but Nate pulls me the other way, inside the back door. I have to wait to test my theory.

After dinner, Nate grabs my harness. I am so excited for this walk that I run at least twenty circles around Nate before he catches me to put on the harness.

When he opens the door, I lunge forward, pulling Nate on a search for a leaf pile. There are none on our street, so we turn onto Edgewood. I see a leaf pile across the street, and I pull Nate in that direction. He obliges, and we cross the street. I run for the leaf pile and dive into it. The leaves move out of my way and collapse around me.

I stop and smile. I am in the middle of the leaf pile. The leaves come up to my neck, but it's okay. I can breathe. There are no sharp or spiky things. The leaves feel great, and a delightful smell fills my nose. The leaf pile is better than the corner light post.

I start kicking, sending the leaves in the air in every direction.

"Zelda, you are getting me dirty," Nate mumbles. I ignore him. Kicking the leaves is so much fun, and the amount of leaf piles on our route is endless. I walk out of the leaf pile. I see another pile a house away. I sprint for it.

Chapter 9
Zelda and Squeaks the Squirrel

Only a few leaf piles remain on the tree lawns in our neighborhood. Every day the breeze becomes a little colder, so I know winter is around the corner.

With winter on its way, I try to spend most of my day outside kicking leaf piles and taking walks. The squirrels are busy collecting nuts in the trees at the far edge of the yard. Some days I lie in the grass and watch them jump from branch to branch, wishing I could join their fun.

I notice a new squirrel scent in the backyard. The squirrel scents are concentrated along the tree line on the far edge of our backyard. This scent, however, is not along the tree line. I smell one squirrel in two new spots–

behind our garage and at the oak tree bordering the patio. I wonder why the squirrel dared to wander into my territory on its own.

My curiosity takes over me, so I change my backyard habits to investigate the mysterious squirrel. When I go outside, I run to the edge of the backyard looking for the squirrel. So far, I haven't had any luck, so I begin watching for the squirrel through the kitchen window. An hour into my stakeout, I notice something brown and fluffy in the oak tree.

Squirrel!

I stand with my front paws on the windowsill, observing the squirrel's every move. When I hear a car pull into the driveway, I know it's the perfect opportunity. I run to the back door. Moments later, Ben opens the door, and I run outside before they can stop me.

"Zelda, no!" Ben says. It's too late. I dash to the oak tree in the backyard. I am ten pug steps away when the squirrel runs from the tree to the ground. I chase after the squirrel, but I can't catch him before he darts up a tree. I gaze at the squirrel on his perch on top of the branch, and he starts squeaking and screeching. I bark and kick the ground.

"Zelda, come!" Nate yells. He steps toward me with a bag of treats.

Treats! Forget the squirrel!

I sprint to Nate, and he gives me a few treats. We walk inside. After enjoying my snack, I remember the squirrel. I walk to the back window and look out, but he is gone.

After our encounter, I name the squirrel Squeaks. I look for Squeaks day and night, inside and outside. I sit on the kitchen chair, staring out the window for any signs of him. Most days, I fall asleep on my chair midway through the day. Today I am determined to stay awake. I sit in my chair, scanning the yard for movement.

When a flash of brown appears in the corner of my eye, I squint, focusing on the brown flash. Squeaks runs down the oak tree, toward the garage. I can't see Squeaks when he moves behind the garage, but he only stays behind the garage for a moment. Then he runs back to the oak tree. Squeaks repeats the pattern five times, and then he disappears into the woods.

I have no idea what he is doing.

When Nate takes me outside later, I pull him to the back of the garage. I follow Squeaks' scent to a small pile of acorns–Squeaks' secret acorn stash. I have an important decision to make.

Is Squeaks a friend or foe?

I break for the oak tree, dragging Nate behind me. I find an acorn, scoop it into my mouth, and run to the stash next to the garage. I place the acorn in the pile and run back to the tree. I grab another acorn; I bring it back to the stash. I place my third acorn in the pile before Nate grows tired of walking in circles with me. He leads me inside.

Over the next two days, I add more and more acorns to the stash. My family catches on to my routine. They let me stay outside longer, so I can collect more acorns.

"Why is Zelda collecting acorns?" Lucy asks.

"Because Zelda thinks she is a squirrel," Nate says.

"Zelda is a little pug. Why does she think she is a squirrel?" Lucy asks.

"I don't know dear," Nate says. Lucy asks more questions, and I know my family thinks I am crazy or confused.

A few days later, I spot Squeaks from my kitchen chair. I scratch at the front door, and Hannah leashes me. My excitement is so high to see Squeaks that I sprint for the backyard with my leash trailing behind me. I turn the corner to the back of the house. Squeaks sits at the bottom of the tree. He runs for the tree line. I am disappointed and out of breath, so I stop running. Squeaks disappears into the woods. I return inside with Hannah, sad I didn't meet Squeaks.

I sulk and sleep away the next few days. I give up my backyard stakeout, and I ignore the acorn stash. Maybe I am foolish to think Squeaks and I can become friends.

A week later, Squeaks is a distant memory. I meander into the backyard with Hannah to do my business, like any other day. As I look for the perfect spot, Squeaks' scent fills my nostrils. I follow my nose toward the tree line. I hear a squeak and gaze into the tree. Squeaks is perched on a branch above my head with an acorn in his mouth.

Clunk!

The acorn hits me on my forehead wrinkles. Squeaks makes lots of noise.

Is he laughing at me?

I think he is. Squeaks runs across his branch to another tree, darts down the tree, and races back up the tree above my head. I look up to see he has another acorn.

I'm not falling for that twice!

I scamper to the right, and the acorn falls to my left. Squeaks leaps to a nearby tree branch and runs down the trunk. I run to the tree and meet him at the bottom of the trunk. Squeaks and I arrive at the same moment. We look into each other's eyes. I freeze, unsure what to do.

Squeaks makes the first move. He grabs another acorn, runs back up the tree, and finds his place above me. I stay still.

Clunk!

Squeaks makes more noise. I air kick below him, kicking leaves, dirt, and grass everywhere. I hear more squeaking and look above. Squeaks smiles down on me. I smile back and look into Squeaks' eyes. He returns the eye contact, and I know we are not enemies–we are friends.

"Zelda, time to go inside," Hannah yells. I bark a goodbye to Squeaks and trot back inside.

Chapter 10
A Pug Christmas Story

The trees are bare, the air is cold, and the cool breeze creates an uncomfortable chill. The sun shines for less of the day. The crunchy morning grass and the frozen puddles on the edge of the yard signal a sad truth. Winter is here.

With my short hair and small body, I am not built for winter weather. I return from walks with a nasty case of the chills, so my time outdoors is limited. Luckily, I have Ben and Lucy to keep me busy. My favorite indoor toy is the purple owl. The owl has the loudest squeaker. To top it off, the wings of the owl crinkle. I love playing with it.

As usual, I take my afternoon nap while the family is gone. I wake up mid-afternoon to the front door opening. I awake to greet Hannah, Ben, and Lucy.

"Ben, grab Zelda," Hannah says. Ben scoops me into his arms as Hannah opens the front door. Nate walks in carrying a pine tree bigger than him. He places the tree in front of the big window in the living room.

I have seen flowers and small plants indoors before, but never a full-size tree. I search my brain for a reason to plant a tree inside our home, and the only idea that pops in my head is squirrels. Maybe we are getting a pet squirrel?

I walk over to the tree and sniff for clues. My sniffs turn to sneezes instantly. I back away. The treetop almost touches the ceiling. Compared to the trees outside, it's a small tree, but in our home, the tree looks huge. The sneezing fit passes, so I smell for squirrel scents. I find no trace of squirrel.

Hmmm...

A few minutes later, Nate brings boxes from the basement, cluttering the living room. Hannah, Nate, Ben, and Lucy spend the next hour playing with the tree. First, they wrap strings with colorful lights around the tree. Next they place balls, other objects, and tiny statues on the tree. Everything they place on the tree resembles a toy.

"Does Zelda have an ornament?" Ben asks.

"Here it is," Nate says and hands something small to Ben. He hangs it on the tree, but it's hanging so high on the tree that I can't see it.

I examine the tree a second time. My sneezes and itchy nose return. I find a little man with a red hat, red coat, and a long white beard hanging within my reach. I stand on my hind legs and use the windowsill to keep my balance. I knock the little red man with my paw and he falls to the ground. I grab him with my mouth and run to Lucy.

"Hi Zelda," Lucy says. "Mom, Zelda has something."

"Zelda, what is that?" Hannah asks. "Nate, can you help me out? I think Zelda has Santa."

"Maybe Zelda is trying to tell Santa what she wants for Christmas," Nate replies with a grin.

"Zelda, drop it," Nate says. Compelled by his command, I drop the statue on the floor.

"This isn't a toy," he says. Nate picks up the statue and places it back on the tree above my reach.

I find a small, shiny red ball hanging low on the tree. I grab it and bring it to Ben.

"Zelda, give me that," Ben says. I run away, and he chases me.

"Mom, Zelda has another ornament," Ben yells in between breaths.

"Get it from her Ben. She can't have them," Hannah yells.

"I'm trying," Ben shouts.

I run in circles until Ben pins me in a corner.

"I have you now!" Ben reaches for me. I squirm furiously to avoid his reach, but in the process, I drop the red ball.

"Ah hah!" Ben says. "I got it Mom!"

"Thanks dear. Bring it back to the tree. Let's move the ornaments higher so Zelda can't reach them," Hannah says.

"But then I can't reach them either," Lucy says. Her bottom lip is turned up.

"I'm sorry Lucy, but we don't want Zelda to break the ornaments or to hurt herself with one," Hannah says.

"It's not fair," Lucy cries. She walks into her bedroom.

"Not again," Ben says. "Lucy is always crying."

"Be nice to your sister," Nate says. "She's young. You cried a lot at that age too."

Since I can't play with the tree toys, I run to Ben with one of my tennis balls. We play until I am tired. I lie on the couch, and I fall asleep.

I awake to some noise outside and an empty house. From my perch on top of the couch, I see a man walking three dogs on the sidewalk. I sprint to the window. I stand up, resting my front legs on the windowsill. I start barking. One of the three dogs sees me and barks back. The other two dogs follow his lead.

I race to the other side of the tree to get a different view. I stand on the windowsill, but my front feet slip. I plummet into the tree. I hear something hit the floor, but I ignore it. I stand again on the windowsill, searching for the dogs. They are out of sight. Bummed, I step down to the floor. A tiny statue of a boy rests under the tree.

I pick it up. It's a little hard for a toy, but it will work. I take it to the back bedroom and bury it in the blanket on the bed next to a milk-bone.

After an afternoon away, my family returns home with bags and boxes. They cover the boxes with colorful paper, put them under the tree, and call them "presents." Over the next week, more presents appear under the tree.

Every day when my family leaves, I look for another toy to gather for my growing collection of tree toys. I stand on the presents to knock down the toy from the tree. I take the fallen tree toy to a hiding spot.

So far, I have a small red ball, a small green ball, one little boy, and one little girl. I hide the toys in my favorite milk-bone spots. I have one in my crate under a blanket, one sandwiched between pillows on the couch, and two under the blanket in the spare bedroom.

"Hey Zelda, what are you doing?" Ben asks when he arrives home that afternoon. I am digging under the pillow in the living room. I stop, scared Ben will discover my secret. Hannah joins us in the living room.

"Ready for Christmas Eve dinner?" Hannah says to the family.

"Yes Mom. Can we bring Zelda?" Ben says.

"Sure, why not? My family loves Zelda."

We spend the evening with Hannah's family. I love their home, especially when I know the visit is short. I run and sniff all corners of the house while the family eats, drinks, and laughs together. When we return home, I head straight for bed and drift to sleep.

I hear Hannah and Nate wake up early the next morning. They are normally slow to get out of bed, but not this morning. I get up from Lucy's bed and follow them into the living room, careful not to wake Lucy. Hannah and Nate put more presents under the tree and as they finish, Ben and Lucy come downstairs. The whole family gathers around the tree. They pass each other the presents and open them one by one. They smile and laugh throughout the entire process.

"Zelda, do you want your Christmas present?" Ben asks.

Ben grabs a big sock hanging on the wall and places it in front of me. I walk over and sniff it. Inside, I see something green. I stick my paw in the stocking and try to get it out. The green thing is stuck in the stocking, but I wedge my paw in the stocking and move it to me. As I put pressure on the green thing, it squeaks.

I recognize that sound!

I move it a little further, so I can grab it with my mouth. I pull out a brand new green owl with a perfect squeaker. I run sprints with it through the house. I bring it to Ben, and we play tug of war.

"What is this?" Hannah asks.

"Huh?" Nate says.

"Come here Nate," Nate walks over to Hannah.

"Look at this," she says. She lifts the pillow on the couch to reveal the small green tree ball hidden next to a milk-bone.

"Zelda hid this ornament here," she said.

Hannah found my hiding spot. I'm in trouble.

"So our pug hides Christmas ornaments?" Nate asks with a big smile.

"I guess so," says Hannah chuckling. "I wonder if we will find any more around the house."

"Probably. Oh well, it's Christmas," Nate says.

"That it is," Hannah says. She leans over and kisses Nate.

"What would you like for Christmas breakfast?" Nate asks.

"Pancakes!" Hannah says. Nate goes into the kitchen and begins cooking breakfast. I follow him into the kitchen. Maybe he will drop some pancake pieces or bacon on the floor. If not, it's still a great morning. I have a new owl, and I didn't get in trouble for hiding the tree toys. But I still have no idea why we have a giant pine tree in our living room!

Chapter 11

Zelda vs. the Snowman

"**D**ad, it's snowing!" Ben shouts. Lucy and I are in bed, wrapped in warm blankets. With winter in full swing, I stay under the blankets most of the day.

"I wonder how Zelda will react to the snow," Nate says to Ben. Nate sits on the couch with a mug in his hand.

"She needs to go out. Why don't you take her and find out?" Hannah says from the kitchen. The word "out" sends me running to the front door.

"Okay, let me find some warm clothes," Nate says. I run in circles around Nate while he puts on his shoes, a giant red coat, and something black on his head.

"Are you ready, Zelda?" he asks. My tail bounces from one side to the other.

Nate attaches the leash and opens the front door. I dash out the door, onto the porch, and freeze.

White stuff covers the ground and the trees. One step at a time, I walk down the steps from the porch. The white stuff is cold yet soft; my paws sink into it. I am not sure I like the feeling. I turn around, jump up the steps, and scratch at the door.

"Back inside already? Don't like the snow?" Nate says.

Snow. That must be the name for the white stuff.

"I don't think Zelda likes the snow," Nate says. "She took one step and ran inside."

"She has to like the snow. All dogs like snow," Ben says.

"Zelda isn't a normal dog," Hannah shouts from the kitchen.

"Nope, she's better than a normal dog with her wrinkly face, curly tail, and snorts," Ben yells back. He grabs my owl and throws it. I fetch it and bring it to him.

"See Mom, Zelda is a great dog," Ben mutters.

Ben and I play until Lucy wakes up and wanders into the living room. I snuggle with her on the couch and snore the day away.

I wake up later in the day and look out the window. The snow covers the yard, and small drops of snow fall from the sky

How long does this stuff last?

Hannah walks into the living room and sees me gazing out the window.

"Do you want to go for a walk in the snow?" Hannah asks with a book in her hand. No, not really, but I walk to the front door. I can't avoid the snow forever. I have to go out.

"Okay Zelda, I'll take you, let me find your hoodie to keep you warm." Hannah walks over to Vacuum's closet and opens the door. I sprint to the door and bark at Vacuum until Hannah pushes me out of the way and closes the door. In her hand is a pug-sized blue shirt. She grabs me, sliding the shirt over my head and my front paws.

With the shirt on my body, I feel trapped. I squirm, but nothing moves. I'm stuck in it, and I probably look ridiculous. With a big sigh, I walk to the door.

The snow is higher than earlier, almost to my stomach. As I walk, I forget about the coldness of the snow and begin to like its softness. I run through the snow, letting it splash around me. Hannah and I run down the sidewalk together.

We stop at the corner, so I can catch my breath. When I stop moving, a cold wind blows, and I'm thankful for the blue shirt. As we walk back home, my curiosity about the snow grows.

Can I eat it?

I take a quick bite as we walk. The snow melts in my mouth and refreshes my dry throat. I stop for more and more mouthfuls on the way.

I could eat this stuff all day!

When we arrive home, I dash indoors to warm up, but this snow stuff is growing on me.

During the evening, Nate takes me for another walk. The sky is dark, but the snow casts a faint glow, and it's eerily quiet outside. We walk down the street on the sidewalk. The wind is blowing harder than earlier, and when we reach the corner, I'm shivering.

Up ahead, I notice a large shadow in someone's yard. As we approach, the shadow grows into a familiar shape. The shadow is cast from a man, who is almost as tall as Nate. The man is made of snow, but much rounder than

Nate or Hannah. He has stone black eyes and mouth, stick arms, a scarf, and shoes. I don't know who is this man, and I don't want to find out. I spin around to return the way we came.

"Zelda, this way," Nate says. I pull him the opposite way, but Nate resists.

"C'mon girl."

I bark a few times and try again to move in the opposite direction of the shadow.

"Okay, okay," he says. Nate lets me leave the shadow. We scurry home.

"How was your walk?" Hannah asks as we walk in the door.

"A little short, but I think Zelda was cold, and she may be afraid of a snowman," Nate says to Hannah.

"Wait, Zelda, let me take this off," Nate says as he pulls the shirt off me. I lick his hands, find a spot on the couch on top of the fuzzy blanket, and fall asleep.

Suddenly, I am running down the street through the snow. Something is chasing me. I look back as I run, and I see it. The man with stone black eyes glides down the street after me. I try to run faster, but the snow is deep, slowing me down.

"Zelda."

I hear my name and open my eyes. I'm lying on the couch without a snowman in sight. It was a nightmare.

"Sleepy-time," says Lucy. I slowly rise and move to Lucy's bed. I lie under the covers next to her.

I have trouble sleeping that night. I can't stop thinking about the man with black eyes. The man haunts me in my dreams. When sunlight shines through the window the next morning, I am grateful.

Not long after I wake up, Hannah takes me on our morning walk. I lead her on the same route as the previous night. At the corner, my heart starts beating faster. I know we are getting close. I continue forward, but at a slower pace. From a distance, I see the white mounds rising out of the ground.

I stop several feet in front of the man. His white body glimmers in the daylight and his black eyes pierce into me. I start barking.

"Zelda, it's okay, it's just a snowman," Hannah whispers. "He can't hurt you."

I want to believe Hannah, but my instincts tell me otherwise. I back away from the snowman. Hannah walks to the snowman and touches his body with her hand. The snowman doesn't move an inch.

"Cmon, girl, it's okay," she says. I walk closer and closer. I take bites of snow along the way. I can't help it; I eat when I'm nervous.

The snowman stands motionless, and with Hannah's reassurance, I take a few more steps. I am next to the snowman. I take a bite of the snowman's belly. The snow is delicious and refreshing.

Wait a minute, I just bit the snowman!

I take one step backward, scared of the snowman's reaction. The snowman's black eyes stare at me, but he doesn't move.

I inch closer. No movement. I am standing next to the snowman. I know I shouldn't, but I can't stop myself. The snow looks so delicious.

I take a bite of the snowman, then another bite, and another, and another.

"Zelda, leave it! Stop eating the snowman!" Hannah says in between laughs. She pulls me away from the snowman, back to the sidewalk. I run forward and lead the way, stopping for mouthfuls of snow or a good scent. When we return home, I curl up on the couch. I won't have nightmares tonight, just sweet dreams of eating a giant snowman.

Chapter 12
Zelda vs. Jack Jack

"**A**re you ready to go see Tucker and Whitney?" Nate asks.

I run to the door with my tail wagging. I can't wait to spend time with Tucker and Whitney again. Tucker and Whitney live with Nate's parents. I met them for the first time a few months ago, and since then, I have been itching to return.

I love hanging out with other dogs, and I also love Tucker and Whitney's house. The downstairs has a long hallway for playing fetch, and the food is great. The best part is the fenced yard. I can go outside and run around without a leash.

Nate loads up a few bags for our visit while Hannah gets Lucy and Ben settled in the back seat of the car. I hop in the back seat with them. It's a long car ride, so I don't try to stay awake. I curl up and fall asleep, anxious to awake at Tucker and Whitney's house.

When I wake up, I am in Lucy's lap. She is sleeping, so I move to Ben's lap and look out the window. We are surrounded by other cars, and I don't know how much longer we will be on the road. I try to fall asleep again, but my heart is pounding with excitement. I stand on the front window and watch the cars.

When Nate turns us off the highway, I know we are close to our destination. We wind through the neighborhood and pull into the driveway. I jump from one side of the car to the other waiting for someone to open the door.

"Zelda, chill," Ben says.

"Ow," Lucy says when I land on her lap. Lucy opens the door.

"Lucy, no, Zelda isn't on her leash!" Ben yells. I jump out of the car and sprint to the front door.

Tucker and Whitney are waiting inside for me, barking like crazy.

"Hi Zelda," Nate's mom says. She opens the door. I run inside, and Tucker runs out. He jumps and licks the whole family, one at a time, while I jump on Nate's dad. He picks me up, and I lick his face.

The rest of my family walks inside, and I run straight to the toy basket and find a ball. I bring it to Ben. Soon Whitney and Tucker join the fun.

After an hour of playing, Tucker, Whitney, and I are spent. I rest on the couch with the crew. My eyes begin to droop, and I am almost asleep when something catches my eye.

In the hallway, near the steps, I see a hint of black fur peeking around the corner. I get up and walk over to the steps to check it out. Nothing is there–maybe I was dreaming. I return to my spot on the couch and relax for the rest of the night.

In the middle of the night, I hear a scratching noise in the hallway. Ben and I are in bed with the door shut. I get up and stand next to the door. The scratching is on the other side of the door, and the scent isn't Whitney's or Tucker's.

What is it?

I jump back on the bed and walk on top of Ben to wake him. He makes a noise, but he doesn't move. I try again, and he stirs.

"Zelda, what do you want?" Ben mumbles. I jump off the bed and walk to the door. "No, Zelda, it's time to sleep." Ben rolls over, and he is asleep again. I wait by the door and listen. The scratching stopped, so I jump back on the bed.

I spend the next morning searching the house for the source of the scratching noise. I start in the basement, inspecting every nook and cranny. I don't find anything unusual.

I head up the stairs and search the main floor, but I don't expect to find anything. Nothing would hide on the main floor with all the traffic and action. I creep upstairs and turn toward the gated room. I sneak around the corner and look through the gate. Sitting on top of a desk is a skinny black cat.

A cat! There's a cat here! A cat! I need to catch it!

I bash into the gate and try to knock it down. It isn't moving. I look at the gate. Maybe I can make the jump. I back up and go for it. As I lift off, I realize this is a bad idea. I can't make the jump. But it's too late, and I smash into the gate and tumble to the ground. I shake off my fall and bark at the cat. The cat sits still, glaring in my direction.

"Zelda, leave Jack Jack alone," Nate commands from the corner of the stairs. I'm confused.

Where was Jack Jack on my last visit? And why is he gated in a room?

"Let's go downstairs," Nate says. I follow Nate.

Later in the evening, I sneak away from the family and creep up the stairs. I peer into the gated room, but I see no sign of Jack Jack. I slip into our bedroom and look. Nothing. I walk down the hall, and I catch a faint glimpse of a new smell that has to be Jack Jack. My nose guides me to the opposite side of the house to Nate's parents' bedroom.

I see a hint of black peeking around the corner of the bed. Stealth isn't a strength of pugs, but I try my best to move quietly. As I inch closer, I know it is Jack Jack. He is distracted by something on the ground. His paw is swatting at a feather. He is playing with the feather, and he has no idea of my approach. I know sneaking up on a cat is a bad idea, but I have to try.

I am a foot or so away when I feel the urge.
I can't hold it in!

The huge sneeze showers Jack Jack with snot and alerts him to my presence. He turns to face me and his fur puffs up.

How do cats do that?

Jack Jack hisses at me.

I have experienced enough cat altercations to know what's coming next. It is the swat. I turn and sprint down the stairs before Jack Jack has the opportunity. I jump on the couch between Tucker and Whitney, hoping they will protect me.

I wait, but Jack Jack doesn't come down the stairs. I know he is waiting for me to return, so I won't go upstairs alone.

I manage to avoid Jack Jack for the rest of the visit, and the next day we return home. I hope he forgets about the sneezing incident. Otherwise, I need to learn some cat defense skills before I visit Tucker and Whitney again.

Epilogue
Zelda vs. Gannondorf

Since Hannah, Nate, Ben, and Lucy adopted me, I have experienced many adventures, protected my family, and learned how to become a well-behaved pug. I conquered the leaf pile, Vacuum, a snowman, and Squeaks the squirrel.

My most terrifying adventure was a tapeworm named Gannondorf. Gannondorf arrived suddenly and quietly one day, causing me terrible pain for several days. Usually, I protect my family, but this time, they saved me.

This story of Gannondorf started on a day like any other. I woke up, went for my morning walk, played for a bit, and took my mid-morning nap while the family went away for the day. I woke up that evening to the door opening.

"Hi Zelda, do you need to go out?" Nate asked.

The rest of the family walked through the door. When I started moving to meet Nate at the front door, my stomach seared with pain. The pain was terrible, but I needed to go out, so I fought through the pain and went outside with Nate. I quickly did my business and returned inside to lie next to Lucy on the couch. I tried to jump onto the couch, but I was too weak. I missed the couch and toppled backward to the floor.

"Do you need some help?" Lucy asked. I looked at her with my sad pug eyes. She picked me up and set me in her lap. I curled up next to her and fell asleep.

I woke up to the sunlight seeping through the curtains. My body was in serious pain. I realized I was in Lucy's bedroom, but I didn't remember moving to the bedroom the previous night. I let out a moan of frustration.

"Morning Zelda," Lucy said. She started to massage my body, but I moved out of her reach.

"Zelda, do you want to go out?" Lucy whispered. I didn't move. "Okay, guess not," she said. I was drained. I closed my eyes and fell asleep.

Lucy was out of bed when I opened my eyes again. I couldn't hold it any longer, so I walked to the front door and sat. I hoped going outside would make me feel better.

"Okay, let's go out," Hannah said from the kitchen. She put on her shoes and coat. We went to the backyard and returned inside. I settled in my dog bed and tried to get comfortable. Every way I turned, my stomach throbbed with pain. I didn't know what to do, and my body shook with terror.

"Why are you shaking Zelda?" Hannah asked. She walked over and pet me. Her soft touch calmed my tremors. I allowed my eyes to close.

I woke up with no sense of how much time had passed. I didn't feel any better. Hannah sat in the chair across from me in the living room. I curled up next to her. The movement caused the pain to worsen, and my tremors returned.

"Zelda, what's wrong?" Hannah asked. I looked at her and tried to show her my pain with my sad, listless eyes.

The next time I woke up Nate, Ben, and Lucy were home. Nate greeted me with a friendly hello and pet. I started shaking again. I couldn't stop myself.

"I think we should take her to the vet," he said to Hannah.

"Me too," Hannah said. "I'll call now." She walked into the other room and returned a few minutes later. "We have a four o'clock appointment."

"Great. We better get moving!" Nate replied. We loaded up into Nate's car, and I felt a glimmer of hope. I loved car rides and maybe we were going somewhere to make me feel better.

When we stopped, I hurried to get out of the car. I sprinted towards the door, and then I stopped dead in my tracks. I recognized the building. The last time I was here I left in pain with six fewer teeth. I was not going inside again. Nothing good happened here.

"Let's go, Zelda," Nate said. I stood frozen to the sidewalk. "C'mon, the vet is going to help you feel better." I didn't want to believe him, but I didn't have any other choice. I followed them inside.

When I walked inside, the variety of animal smells overwhelmed me, and for a minute, I forgot why I was there. I let my nose guide me around the room until Nate led me down a hallway into a room with a woman in a white coat. They talked with each other, but I didn't recognize many of the words.

"It's okay, Zelda," said Nate. Nate handed the white coat woman a bag.

"I'll be back in a few minutes with a diagnosis," the white coat woman said. Nate picked me up from the counter and placed me in his lap. I wanted this nightmare to be over. I lay down and closed my eyes until I heard the door open.

"Zelda has a tapeworm. I am writing a prescription to cure her. She will be back to normal in a day or two," the white coat said.

"Thanks so much," Nate replied. The white coat said goodbye and left.

"Did you hear that Z? You are going to be fine." Nate said. I hoped Nate was right. We returned to the rest of the family in the big room.

"What's wrong?" Ben asked anxiously.

"Zelda has a tapeworm. She will take medicine and be back to normal in a couple of days," Nate said.

"Oh good," Hannah replied.

"We should call the tapeworm Gannondorf," Ben said.

"What? Why?" Hannah asked.

"Because Gannondorf was the villain in the Zelda video games," he replied.

"Oh yeah, I remember now." Hannah turned to me, "Don't worry Zelda, we will help you vanquish the evil tapeworm Gannondorf."

I didn't recognize some of the words Hannah said to me, but I think I understood the message. My family had a plan to save me from Gannondorf, and then I would be back to my normal walking, playing, and sneezing pug-self.

At home, Nate called me to the kitchen. When I walked into the kitchen, I smelled something delicious.

Peanut butter!

I love peanut butter. Maybe that's what will make me feel better!

Nate knelt next to me with peanut butter covering his finger. He signaled for me to eat it, and I didn't hesitate. The peanut butter was delicious. I was in heaven. But I noticed something small in the peanut butter. It was hard and tasted bad. I stopped licking the peanut butter.

"C'mon Zelda, you need to eat it, it will make you better," Nate said. He slopped more peanut butter on his finger and called me over. I stared at him.

Is this part of the plan to save me from Gannondorf?

I took a deep breath and forced the gross food down my throat. I swallowed, drank some water, and reclaimed my spot on the couch.

I slept through the night and woke up with the sun in the morning. I stood on the bed and waited for the pain to return. No pain! I walked to the other side of the bed and stood on Lucy to wake her. I felt discomfort, but nothing like the past few days. I sneezed and licked Lucy's face.

"Good morning," she said. I walked to Ben's bedroom and jumped on him. He grumbled at first, but then he pet me.

"Do you want to go for a walk?" Ben asked. I ran to the front door.

"It's good to see Zelda prevailed over Gannondorf the tapeworm," Hannah said with a grin on her face. I waited by the door with squirrels on my mind.

Gannondorf taught me an important lesson about my family. As a pug, I knew my responsibility was to protect my family, but it's a great feeling knowing my family watches over and cares for me too.

A Sneak Preview from
The Adventures of Zelda:
The Second Saga

I can't believe a year has passed since my family adopted me. The past year was filled with every sort of adventure. I conquered Vacuum, the leaf pile, and the skate park. I became friends with Tucker, Whitney, and Squeaks; I survived attacks from Jack Jack, the Snowman, and Gannondorf. Although the excitement has waned in the past few weeks, I know another adventure will cross my path soon.

My new adventure arrived a week ago with the appearance of boxes. Boxes usually live in the basement, but for the past week, they have multiplied into every room of the house. I have no idea what is inside the boxes. Most of them are closed, and I am too short to see in them, even when standing on my hind legs. The worst part is they are taking up most of the floor. My pug sprints are contained to a small circle around the coffee table in the living room. Pug sprints are not supposed to be contained to small spaces.

After a week of the boxes piling up, they begin to disappear almost as quickly and quietly as they appeared. Nate and Hannah have been carrying the boxes to the car. Hannah and Nate return later, but not the boxes.

Where are the boxes going? I hope I don't end up in one of them!

The boxes are a mystery, and I know I am the right pug to solve it. With only a few boxes remaining in the living room, I have a limited amount of time. I need a quick, decisive plan. One of the remaining boxes is open and next to the couch. I hop onto the couch and look inside the box. I don't see anything sharp or spiky, so I back up, get a running start, and jump into the box. I land on a hard, slippery surface and slide into the other side. I gather myself and use my paw to shut one flap of the box. I lie underneath it to conceal myself.

I start to fall asleep in the box when I hear Nate coming my way. My heart starts beating faster as I think about where Nate might take the box and me. My nerves get the best of me, and the hiccups start.

Nate is going to find my hiding spot!

But Nate never picks up my box. I hear him turn around and walk in the opposite direction.

I breathe a sigh of relief, my heartbeat slows, and my hiccups dissipate. When I hear footsteps a second time, I am as silent and motionless as a stone. Nate picks up the box. But the box is crooked. I slide in the opposite direction, crashing into the other side.

"Zelda, what are you doing in here?" he asks. I bark, trying to signal my intention to go with him. He puts the box down, lifts me up, and puts me on the ground.

"It's not time for you to go yet," he says. "But soon, Z. Hang in there." Nate lifts the box and carries it outside. I am so frustrated and disappointed that I lie right where Nate put me. I close my eyes and fall asleep.

I wake up to movement and voices.

"We need to lock Zelda up so she doesn't get trampled," Hannah says.

"She's not going to like that," Ben says.

"I know, but it needs to happen. Why don't you put her in the crate for the next few hours?" Hannah replies. Before I realize what is happening, Ben is carrying me. He puts me in the crate in the corner of the room. I bark a few times, but I know it's pointless; I heard Hannah's words.

I watch the action from inside the crate. It's chaos. Everything is in motion—the couch, chairs, people, and boxes. I have never seen anything like it. I can't see where anything is going, but I assume it is out the door.

I lose track of time, entranced by the scene in front of me. When Ben finally lets me out of the crate, the living room has transformed. There is nothing left in it except my crate, food bowl, and water dish. I don't even have any toys.

What is going on?

"Zelda, we will be back for you in a few hours," Ben says. He walks over and pets me before leaving out the front door. I walk to the window and see Ben walk into a big white and orange truck. I explore the other rooms of the house and find the same scene. Every room is empty—no beds, chairs, or bookcases. I return to the living room and look out the window, hoping Lucy and Ben will be outside waiting for me. They aren't.

I walk toward my crate to lie down, and then I notice the closet door is open a crack. I paw the door completely open; Vacuum is staring back at me. I immediately bark twice at her.

I am not scared of Vacuum since I tore her arm off, but we are not on good terms. I don't trust her. I constantly remind her that I am the head of the family.

Why would they leave me alone with Vacuum?

I walk over to my crate and lie down. I am completely stumped; I don't know what to do or what is happening. I go back over the conversation from earlier. Ben said they would be back for me. He wouldn't lie, and my family wouldn't leave me behind. I start to close my eyes, but I see Vacuum out of the corner of my eye.

What about Vacuum?

As much as I don't like Vacuum, I know they can't leave her behind, either. It wouldn't be right. She's been with the family almost as long as I have. She is a bit of a bully. On the other hand, she adds mystery and adventure to my life.

I know what I need to do.

I get up and walk over to Vacuum. I bark once to let her know I'm on her side. Then I grab one of her arms and start pulling her toward my crate, but she topples over onto the ground.

Whoops.

I grab her arm again and start pulling. She's heavier than I remember, but I have enough strength. After an exhausting few minutes,

Vacuum is next to my crate. I tell her to get up, but she doesn't listen, and after a few minutes of trying, I give up. There is no way I can get her standing again.

I walk into my crate and lie down. It was exhausting work, but hopefully my family will understand.

I wake up to the front door opening.

"Zelda, it's time to go to your new home," Hannah says. I dart to her and greet her with a lick to the face to show my appreciation for her return. "It's good to see you, too."

"What happened here?" she asks, walking to Vacuum. "Did you get mad at the vacuum again?" she says with a laugh. "Okay, let's get you loaded up."

Hannah takes my crate, food bowl, and water dish to her car. She returns inside and grabs my leash. I run over to Vacuum and bark.

"It's time to go," Hannah says, coming toward me with the leash. I dart away, and she follows me. I sprint back to Vacuum and grab her arm, pulling her toward the door.

"No, Zelda, leave it," Hannah says. I can't mess up my chance to leave with Hannah, so I obey against my instincts. I slowly walk to the door. Hannah leashes me, and we go for a ride, leaving Vacuum behind.

Should I have done more?

The ride is surprisingly short. We pull into the driveway of an unfamiliar house. The big truck is there, along with Nate's black car. I jump out of the car, and Hannah leads me up the front steps.

"Hi, Z Bug," Lucy says as I enter the house. She bends over and gives me a pet on my forehead wrinkles. I sneeze in her face; for some reason, petting my forehead always makes me sneeze.

"C'mon, I will show you our new house." Lucy takes the leash from Hannah.

Lucy leads me through the house—the living room, dining room, kitchen, and bedrooms. This house has two stairways! One stairway goes down; the other goes up. I recognize much of the stuff in the house—my couch and chair, the beds, and the boxes. The house is bigger than the last—so much more room for pug sprints. I can't wait to try it out when the boxes disappear.

After our tour, Lucy takes me back to the living room. Hannah and Nate are sitting together on the couch, and Ben's in the chair. I jump into Nate's lap.

"Welcome to your new home, Zelda," Nate says. Mystery solved. The boxes and I are in a new home. I reach up and lick Nate's face.

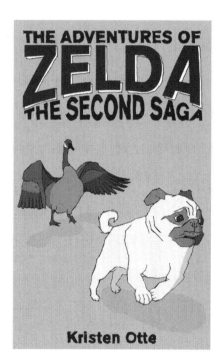

Available Now!

AFTERWORD

Thank you for purchasing this book. Zelda's adventures continue in *The Adventures of Zelda: The Second Saga* and *The Adventures of Zelda: Pug and Peach*.

If you enjoyed this book, please leave a review at Amazon or Goodreads. In addition, I invite you to visit my website and join my email list to receive updates on my latest writing projects.

In addition, I want to thank a few people who were big supporters of this project. First, thanks to my family for supporting my writing career and everything I do. A special thanks to my mother who constantly reminds me of the proper place to put commas and proofreads my work. Another special thanks to Elspeth Peterjohn for her encouragement and for proofreading the collection. Thanks to Michael McFarland for designing an awesome cover. Thanks to my husband, Brian, for not thinking I am crazy for pursuing a career in writing. And finally, thanks to our pug, Zelda, for inspiring these stories and bringing joy and laughter into our home.

ABOUT THE AUTHOR

Author Kristen Otte writes books for children, teens, and adults. Her mission is to bring joy and laughter through stories to people young and old. When she isn't writing or reading, you may find her on the basketball court coaching her high school girls' team. If she isn't writing or coaching, she is probably chasing her husband and dogs around the house.

BOOKS BY KRISTEN OTTE

The Adventures of Zelda: A Pug Tale
The Adventures of Zelda: The Second Saga
The Adventures of Zelda: Pug and Peach
The Adventures of Zelda: The Four Seasons
The Photograph
The Evolution of Lillie Gable

Learn more about Kristen, her books, and her workshops at her website:
www.kristenotte.com.

Made in the USA
San Bernardino, CA
05 May 2016